LOVING THE WRONG MAN

BOOK 1

MIA BLACK

B ack in Charlotte

I'VE HEARD a lot of people say that before they commit a crime of passion, they see black or red before taking matters into their own hands. However, me being the weirdo that I am, saw a lovely shade of zinnia pink as I opened the door and walked in on the love of my life getting sloppy toppy from our next-door neighbor. This lovely shade of pink enveloped the furniture and the walls of my home, obscuring my sense of sight; however, I could still feel, hear, and smell everything. I heard Aaron get up and scream,

"Baby, oh my God. What are you doing here so early???"

In my current state of blindness, I stumbled and felt around for anything that I could throw in his direction. No. Such. Luck. I still couldn't see, and the pink haze continued to surround me. Maybe it was God saying that this wasn't the time to end Aaron's life, because He knew that if I could see properly, Aaron would've been a goner. My next-door neighbor, Tracy, however, wasn't so lucky. An open-palmed slap jolted me out of my carnation-hued stupor, and my eyes refocused on this half-naked slut in her dirty Family Dollar bra and panties. "No this bitch did not just slap me.... Did she forget that I'm from Chicago?" I thought to myself.

I ducked as she tried to swing at me again, and as I came back up, I twisted my fingers into her tacky-ass weave. I brought her head down and cracked her nose against my knee. I lifted her head up as she cried and turned her towards Aaron, who sat dumbfounded in the corner chair. "So this is how you do me? With my homegirl, the next-door neighbor?"

"Baby, I..." Aaron said, not knowing

whether to laugh or to plead with me. Either way, I wasn't having it.

"Nigga, don't baby me. Mothafucka, you're NEXT!!!" I twisted Tracy's arm behind her and dragged the bitch toward the door, bloody nose and all. As she struggled against me, I whispered to her, "I always wondered how a broke bitch like you could live here with no job. I see you been selling mouth. Cheap ass bitch." I opened my front door and threw her half-naked ass right out into our front yard. Before closing the door, I yelled, "Now other niggas can really see what else you working with, nasty slut bitch."

I slammed the door behind me and headed toward the den. If Aaron was smart, he would have already packed up some of his shit and left this house. However, he was never one that had too much common sense. Sure enough, as I predicted, he was still in the den, sitting in the chair.

"This nigga is really foolhardy," I thought to myself as he scrambled to pull on his pants. "Dumb nigga, dumb nigga, DUMB nigga!!" I called out to him as I stood in the doorway. Trying to fight back tears, I looked at him with pity and asked this one question: "Why?"

Aaron looked down at the ground and then back up at me. He shrugged his shoulders and said, "Because."

I looked at all of the weapons within reach, the lamp, the chair, the African spears on the wall. It took all of my power not to pick up one of them spears and harpoon him like a whale. Then I looked into his money-green eyes, the same ones I fell in love with a year and half ago, and felt a strange calm come over me. Straightening up my posture and flicking my hair over my shoulder, I walked into the den. As I was walking past him, he reached out to grab me. I pushed him back down into the chair.

"Stay there," I growled and walked into the bedroom.

I went into the closet and pulled out his suitcase. I calmly went to each drawer, took out his clothes and placed them neatly into the suitcase. When Aaron realized what I was doing, he ran over to me and wrapped his arms around my waist.

"Baby, please. I am sorry. I don't know what came over me. It just happened."

"I didn't know that your dick ending up in someone's mouth just happened, but hey, this is the south. Y'all do shit differently than us northerners."

Aaron continued to hug me. I shrugged him off. "Please get off of me, Aaron."

Aaron let me go and stepped back as I walked past him to our bathroom. I pulled every single toiletry the man had from our shelves and, with arms full, dumped them into his suitcase. He just stared at me as I worked. After stuffing as much of his clothes as I could into his suitcase, I lugged it off the bed and walked towards the front room, through the front door and sat it upright in the front yard. I reached back into the house and put his car keys on top of the travel bag. By then, Aaron had put on his University of North Carolina hoodie and was walking towards the doorway. He looked at me again.

"Jazmine, baby, we can work this out. I really don't—"

I put my hand up to stop him. I stepped toward him, our lips almost touching. I whispered to him, "Now I've been as calm as I possibly could about this, but I am not above making a scene. Now if you don't want your manhood questioned, I suggest you get the fuck out of this house and go over to Tracy's. If you can make a home in her mouth or whatever else you been doing with the bitch while I wasn't around, you might as well live with her too. You can also keep the keys as well, because I will change the locks on this mothafucka."

Aaron stepped outside and looked at me. "But my name is on the lease, baby. You can't do that to me."

I snapped my fingers. "Oh yeah, that's right. Only your name is on the lease. However, I was splitting the rent with you. You may still have to live with Tracy because I don't even know how you would be able to handle the rent all by yourself. I'm still changing the locks though. Good day, sir." I slammed the door in his face. My parents always taught me to only cry behind closed doors. "Never let them see you sweat" was my dad's motto, and I would admit that it had served me well in many a confrontation.

I walked into the bedroom and closed all the blinds. I sat down on our bed, unable to hold back the avalanche of tears that came streaming down my face. I had to allow myself these few minutes to grieve, not knowing what I was going to do. I knew I couldn't go back to Chicago, at least not for this reason. My family and friends were flat out against me moving down here for some man who hadn't made his intentions known about making me his wife. Although they loved me, I didn't want to go back home with my tail between my legs just to hear a chorus of I told you sos. As the tears flowed, the blurriness of the last hour began to subside, and I began to see things in a sharper focus. The day, the week, the month, hell, the year had started out so great. I racked my brain to see if there were signs I missed that could have shown me what was going on. I knew I worked hard to get my freelance business off the ground, but it didn't consume me so much that I was never home to attend to Aaron's needs. Or maybe I was that busy.

"Dammit, Jazzy, don't blame yourself for his bullshit," I said to myself.

I leaned back and the memories began to flood. I had met Aaron while I was finishing up my degree at DePaul University. We'd met at 52Eighty. I was with my girls and he was visiting a couple of his cousins who lived on the west side. I felt a pair of eyes drilling a hole in the back of my head. I turned around and my eyes locked with a pair of money-green eyes, framed in a chocolate-brown face. I turned back around and took another drink of my Madras. After a few minutes, I felt a hand gently touch my arm. I turned around and it was him. His eyes were even more gorgeous up close. They drew me in. He smiled at me and slightly licked his lips. I could tell he was nervous.

"Hello, Miss?"

My girl, Anitra, turned around and nudged me.

"Yes?" I said.

"Would you like to dance with me?" he asked, his accented voice slightly trembling. He sounded like he was from the south.

I looked over at the dance floor to the few people dancing. It was maybe a crowd of ten; either way, I was not getting up. I responded.

"No. I'm here with my girls. But thank you for asking." I turned back around.

"I understand." He walked away. I. Can't. Even. Anitra looked at me and smiled.

"Girl, he was cute."

"Yeah, he was, but still, not tonight." I said as I took another sip of my drink. Anitra smiled at me and shook her head. I was all about finishing school and didn't need any distractions, even from something that would probably be a one-time thing. Like old boy over there.

Needless to say, throughout that night, he came up to me two more times. Normally, after the second time, I would have maced old boy or got him kicked out of the club. But his old school southern charm was slowly wearing me down. It was a stark difference from the South Side Chicago boys I was used to. With these negroes out here, even after politely telling them you were not interested, you got called all kinds of bitches and hoes. And my response... Let's just say that in my younger years, I've baptized more than a few faces with Jose Cuervo or Jack Daniels. Now I've grown up and had to be mature.

I was walking out of the ladies' bathroom toward the deejay booth. I was about to call it a night, but I wanted to hear one of my favorite songs before I left. As I made my way to the stage, I felt a hand gently grab mine. I looked up and, sure enough, it was Mr. Southern Hospitality. We stared at each other for a few moments.

"You are a relentless one, aren't you?"

He swallowed hard and licked his lips one

more time. "Miss, if I am getting on your nerves, please let me know. It's just that I am so struck by your beauty that I just at least have to know your name."

I smiled. He was too cute. I rolled my eyes flirtatiously. "I'm Jazmine. And you are?"

He smiled shyly. "My name is Aaron."

"You're not from here, are you, Mr. Aaron?"

"No. I'm from North Carolina."

I winked at him. "Hmmm...a southern boy. I would have never guessed," I said jokingly.

"Charlotte, to be exact."

"I've never been. So what brings you to the windy city?"

"I'm visiting my family."

I nodded and then looked past him toward the deejay booth. I then turned my head back to Aaron. "I'm about to leave, but it's actually refreshing to know that manners still exist. I was going to ask the deejay to play one of my favorite songs before I left. I think I might take you up on that dance offer. That is, if it's still being offered."

He smiled at me and nodded. "It is."

"Then lead the way."

Aaron turned around and, while holding my

hand, led us through the crowd toward the deejay booth. I requested my favorite song, "Gods" by Jaye featuring Ab-Soul. It wasn't a song to really dance to, but I thought it was a good compromise. We could do a little two step on the dance floor and talk. That dance turned into a two-hour conversation and an exchange of phone numbers. The rest, as they say, is history.

Although I had been here for almost a year, I still felt like a fish out of water. It was much slower here. I wasn't used to the looks that the white folks gave me, but my parents had told me this would happen. Ultimately, I had to take the good with the bad. And Aaron made it all worth it, or so I thought. Maybe that was why I felt so out of place, because I was never meant to be here, and Aaron's and Tracy's betrayal cemented the deal.

The prior events of the day also replayed in my mind. When I left home this morning, I had been so excited about my new client, Carancel Digital Arts, which was one of the largest multimedia companies in the Charlotte area. Usually freelancers thrived in major markets such as New York, Los Angeles or my hometown of

Chicago, so I was blessed to have negotiated a one-hundred thousand dollar, year-long contract with benefits and the option to renew at the end of the year. Although I remained solvent for the entire time I'd lived here, my family thought I was crazy for moving down to North Carolina. I was a city girl, and my parents were afraid that I wouldn't become accustomed to the ways of the south, i.e., the racism, but I followed my heart and his name was Aaron.

Through thick and thin, Aaron seemed to be happy for me. He was making his way as a construction supervisor for the local school district. We were on our way to becoming the new Huxtables: black, gifted and well-off. When I got the contract, he took me to the Capital Grille to celebrate. I drove to work today, reveling in the blessings of a great job, family, friends and a good man by my side. I spent most of the day signing the final paperwork and negotiating my schedule and deliverables. I finished early.

My drive home at two in the afternoon was crazy. "Lawd hammercy, I never understood the traffic in Charlotte. I mean I understood it was a large city in the south, but it wasn't on the level of my hometown of Chicago," I thought to myself as I fought through the bumper-to-bumper traffic on Tryon Street. Part of the reason I took the Carancel job was because the main offices were less than five miles away from me. I eventually made my turn onto North Davidson Street, or NoDa as the locals called it. I drove up to our little bungalow and noticed Aaron's car in the driveway. He worked from 6:30 a.m. to 3:30 p.m. Monday through Friday. It was 2:30 p.m.; there was no way that he would be home at this time. As I parked in the driveway and got out of the car, I was hoping that he wasn't sick. Little did I know, my life would change that day…

I opened my eyes as the last two tears rolled down my cheeks and created little puddles on my sheets. I sat up and wiped my eyes. Now it was time to make some moves. I logged into my banking app and checked my available funds. Thank God. I had saved up six months' worth of money. Coupling that with my new contract, I knew I could survive for roughly nine months, which included moving and flying back to Charlotte for Carancel. I had to shake things up and go my own way. I couldn't go back home. I was not going back home. I wanted to ball out; I wanted to be petty and flaunt my success in Aaron's face.

I picked up my MacBook and started to search. Airline booked, a quick call to my girl, apartment interviews lined up, list of potential media companies who were looking for free-lancers. Never underestimate the tenacity of a black woman scorned. After a few hours of reorganizing my life, I began to pack my bags.

"New York, here I come."

CHAPTER 1

Layovers were the worst, but I had to get the quickest flight out of here, and this was all they had at the price I could afford. As I waited to board the next flight, I thought about the last few days. I'd always prided myself on being able to move on quickly and never look back, but I kept getting almost hourly reminders. Hotline Bling remix by Erykah Badu was interrupted by a familiar ringtone. Him again!! How inappropriate. Really nigga? If I haven't answered your phone calls or texts since I kicked you out of the house, you should take the hint. Plus, he had Tracy to keep him warm at night.

I closed my eyes and let the phone ring out.

I could honestly never understand why dudes always cheated with a downgrade. Here I was with long, natural black hair, smooth cocoa-brown skin and hazel eyes. I'd admit, Aaron would sometimes talk out of the side of his neck about what I would eat, but I thought I was thick in all the right places. Plus, I didn't have any twerk videos or thirst trap photos. I was educated, sweet and polite. They supposedly didn't make them like me anymore. However, he went around and stuck it in a shorty who looked like she may bathe maybe twice a week. Tracy was one of them girls that could best be described as basic. She wasn't ugly or anything. She was a little on the thin side, but there was nothing really amazing about her. Maybe those women made men feel more special than what they were. The male ego was a trip sometimes.

I would admit, Tracy had become a good friend of mine over the year that I was in Charlotte, but that was by accident. She did introduce me to some of the amazing parts of the city, as well as gave me someone to hang out with when I wasn't around Aaron. Ultimately, I think our friendship was more based on her being my next-door neighbor and doing her damnedest to reach out to me. I guess it was a North Carolina thing to be so persistent. My phone rang again, and I looked down at the screen. Aaron again. This was getting more pathetic by the minute.

Over the last week, while I was making the final preparations for leaving Charlotte, I thanked God that I didn't really make a lot of big purchase items for our apartment. All I had was my clothes, shoes and accessories. All of those things were able to fit in the same suitcases I used to move down there. My books and other items could be boxed and sent for later. Although I didn't answer his phone calls, I did listen to the fifty-seven voicemails Aaron left. I just wanted to make sure that he didn't say something crazy where I would have to protect myself. His messages were the usual bullshit. One minute he was begging for forgiveness, and in the next message he tried to blame me for his actions. I couldn't stand a wishy-washy-ass man. Just pick a side and stick to it.

They finally called my boarding time. I was in the A segment, so I was one of the first to board. I took my two carry-ons and boarded the plane. I always chose an aisle seat. I utterly hated flying and wanted to sit where I could make a quick escape. It would be just a little under three hours before I touched down in the Big Apple. No phone calls, nothing but air. I was going to do my best to enjoy this. The first thing I was going to do when I settled in was change my number. I was finally going to put it all behind me. The captain announced that this wasn't going to be a full flight while people continued to board the plane. I kept my eyes closed, doing my best to control my breathing. The two parts of flying that scared me the most were takeoff and landing. Friends that used to work for the airlines told me that takeoff and landing were the most dangerous. I always resolved when flying that if it was my time to go, I had lived a pretty good life.

A deep voice interrupted my meditation. "Excuse me miss, but can I sit right here?"

Keeping my eyes closed, I responded, "Sure."

I stood up and opened my eyes to find one of the most handsome men that I ever laid eyes on standing in front of me. He had short, curly black hair, beautiful cinnamon-brown skin and light golden-brown tiger eyes. The contrast of his eyes was absolutely gorgeous against his skin tone. He was exceptionally tall, dwarfing me in comparison. And that wasn't an easy task, because I stood at an easy five foot nine myself. He had the build of a track runner, lean with sinewy muscle. Damn, he was gorgeous.

"I could stare at you all day too, but I think the other passengers might revolt if we keep holding up takeoff," he said, laughing. I smiled awkwardly and moved into the aisle. He sat down in the chair next to me and buckled himself. I sat back down and did the same. I completely had to maintain my composure.

Before I was able to close my eyes and turn on my music, he turned to me and held out his hand. "Since we are going to be seatmates for the next three hours, I should introduce myself. My name is Quinton, but I go by Que for short."

I reached out and shook his hand. "My name is Jazmine."

"Beautiful name for a beautiful woman."

I felt myself blush. "Thank you for the compliment."

"Anything to put a smile on your face. So,

are you going to New York, or is that another layover?"

I was just about to answer him when the captain's voice was heard over the intercom. I went into my special place as the captain's voice droned on about safety measures. Shortly after, I felt the plane back up and position itself to take off. I took a deep breath as the plane accelerated forward and we lifted into the air. I gripped the armrests as I tried my best to control my breathing. I felt Que's hand gently caress mine. I felt my body tingle a little and moved my hand farther down the armrest. He got the hint, and I felt his weight shift next to me. I took a few more deep breaths as the plane aligned itself in the sky.

After a few more moments, Que said, "I didn't mean to be so forward, but I sensed you were nervous, so I wanted to calm you down."

"Thank you, but I do hope you understand. I just met you. I don't let random men touch me." I absolutely hated flying, but unfortunately it was the only quick way to travel long distances. I also hated travelling long distances. So I knew once I got to New York, I had to make it, because I wouldn't be leaving any time soon.

"Well now that you seem a little better, what are you going to do once you get to New York?"

"It's for a change of scenery, both career and otherwise. It's the city that never sleeps, and I have insomnia."

"So, you're a party girl?"

"Not quite. I mean who doesn't like to let their hair loose, but I'm building my business."

"What do you do for work?" Que asked.

"I work as a freelance consultant to multi-media companies. I am a graphic artist. I have a couple Charlotte companies that I work with, but I need to expand myself and New York is where it's at. What about you?"

"I work in sales."

"How is that coming along?"

Que looked away from me and nodded his head. "It's going well. In fact, I was coming from a trade show."

"How did that go?"

"Boring as hell, but it's a part of the job."

"I know how that is."

The stewardess came over and tapped me

on the shoulder. "Ma'am, can I get you something to drink?"

"Can I have a cranberry and vodka?"

"Sure, and you sir?"

Que smiled. "I would like to have what the lady is having."

"Sure sir." The stewardess prepared our drinks and handed them to us. Between sips, we continued our conversation.

"So you always get the girly drinks?" I asked him.

"I didn't know what impression I wanted to give you. I didn't want you to think I'm a drunkard if I order a vodka straight up."

"I would have just thought this man is about his liquor." I laughed as I took another sip. "I needed this to calm down a little more."

"I'm not helping just a little bit?"

I took another sip of my drink and patted his hands. "You are."

Que smiled and leaned back in his chair. "Then my good deed is done for the day. I made a beautiful woman smile."

I blushed and leaned back. I turned on Erykah Badu and closed my eyes, letting her soothing voice lull me to sleep. I had to put some mental distance between Que and me. I just got out of a year-long relationship with a man that I thought I was going to marry. A man I gave up everything for. I wasn't supposed to feel electricity every time this new man looked at me. I wasn't supposed to get goose pimples every time he spoke to me. I wasn't supposed to tingle between my legs every time he moved close to me or touched my arm. I didn't pride myself on being a thirsty broad, but truth be told, sitting next to this fine-ass man made a sista feel a little parched. I was all for a little adventure, and if I wasn't the type of woman I was, this man would have initiated me into the mile-high club. And he knew what he was doing, but I wouldn't allow him to win. My thoughts turned to Aaron and how he did me wrong. Sad thing was, even at the best parts of my relationship with Aaron, I never felt these kind of sensations. Maybe I never really was in love

The captain's voice lulled me out of my meditation. "Ladies and gentlemen, this is your captain speaking. As we start our descent into JFK International, please make sure your seat backs and tray tables are in their full upright position. Make sure your seat belt is securely fastened and all carry-on luggage is stowed underneath the seat in front of you or in the overhead bins. Thank you."

As I returned the tray to its proper position, I caught Que staring at me out of the corner of my eye. I smiled and pulled my chair upright. The plane began to tilt; I began to grip the armrests of my chair. My knuckles were turning yellow. I felt Que shift, and he caressed the back of my hand. I once again felt that tingling sensation in between my thighs. After what seemed like an eternity, our plane landed. When the plane finally stopped, he let go of my hand. I turned to him and he winked. I blushed again.

"On behalf of American Airlines and the entire crew, I'd like to thank you for joining us on this trip, and we are looking forward to seeing you on board again in the near future. Have a nice stay!" The captain's voice was soothing to my ears. I made it through another dreaded airplane ride. I promised myself that I wouldn't be making any more of these any time soon.

Que helped me with my overhead luggage as we exited the plane. We walked in silence through the tunnel toward the baggage claim area. We nodded at each other and then went our separate ways. I took out my cell phone and called my best friend, Tami, who I made arrangements with to stay with while I searched for apartments. She picked up on the second ring.

"Hey girl," Tami said excitedly. "Are you here?"

"Yes, girl. I'm in baggage claim right now, waiting for my last few bags before I come outside. Where are you?"

"I'm circling around. Let me know what gate you're at so I can meet you when you're done."

"I'll let you know. Okay, call you back. Thanks love." I hung up the phone.

Que came up behind me and tapped me on the shoulder. I turned around.

"I thought you left."

"I was about to leave, but I knew I had to get to know you better," Que said.

"Is that right?" I questioned.

"Look, I know you're gonna be busy over the next couple days, getting yourself situated, but I definitely would love to give you a tour of my hometown. Brooklyn has a lot of cool bars and things to do."

"That would be nice."

"Here, take my number."

I took out my phone.

"Seven, one, eight, five, five, five, three, zero, six, four," Que continued.

"Got it." I dialed his number and sent him a text. I heard the ding of his text alert. He pulled his phone out of his pocket and smiled.

"Expect a phone call from me. I'll see you in a couple days, Miss Jazzy."

"Likewise." I smiled. Que gave me a quick hug and made his way out of the airport.

After a few more minutes of waiting, I saw my two lavender suitcases. Hooking them together, I started to make my way out of the airport. Once I was standing outside at the entrance, I dialed Tami again.

"Hey girl. You finally done?"

"Yes I am."

"Which gate are you?"

I looked up and around. "I'm at terminal 7."

"I'll be there in ten minutes."

My girl, Tami, was the yin to my yang. I was

the more reserved one who always had her head in the books. Tami, on the other hand, was my complete opposite. She was wild, sexy and crazy, but she always handled business. She worked for Ernst and Young as an account manager, making over 100,000 dollars a year. She was one of the baddest chicks I knew. She was just what I needed to help me forget and move on. She drove up and parked her 2016 white Benz. She got out of the car and gave me the biggest hug.

"Hey Jazzy. I'm so glad you out here. Girl it's about to be on."

"Hey boo. I know. I missed you too," I said, hugging her back.

"Let's get these bags in the car." Tami reached over and took one of my suitcases. She pressed the button on her key and the trunk opened. We walked to the back of the car and loaded the trunk. When we got inside the car, D'Angelo's new album was playing through the speakers.

"Girl, you sure know how to make a chick feel like she's home," I said as I buckled myself in.

"Jazzy, New York is your home now. They

got a Gino's East here and some fly-ass fellas. That's all you need, girl."

"Honey, it's been less than a week since the breakup. I am hardly thinking about another man right now."

"Nothing wrong with giving yourself some time to get over things, but you can't let the nani grow cobwebs either."

"I'll know when it's the right time." I sighed. The thing was, I didn't know if it would ever be the right time. I was not one to give out my feelings on a whim. I could honestly say that Aaron was the only man that I truly loved. I didn't know if I wanted to make the mistake of letting someone get so close that I uprooted myself again.

As we drove through the boroughs toward Brooklyn, Tami turned down the music and took a deep breath. "I might be joining you."

I turned to her. "Joining me where?"

"At the singles club. Girl, I can't take no more of Jordan's shit. All this nigga do is cheat, and with ratchet bitches. It's downright embarrassing."

My mouth dropped open at the revelation.

Besides being an all-around badass, she was absolutely stunning. With beautiful chocolate-brown skin and dark eyes, she looked like a five-foot-five, curvy, Trinidadian Naomi Campbell. Her hair was always styled to the Gods. As of late, she was rocking her hair straight with subtle red highlights. "How long has this been going on?"

"Shit, I don't even know. Over the two years we've been together, I caught him with about three different girls. They was all some dinosaur-faced-ass bitches too." We laughed. That was Tami's way, to make a joke about a situation when something was really bothering her.

She continued. "But it still hurts. I've been nothing but good to him, and this is how he treats me."

I touched her shoulder. "You're better than this honey. Why do you stay?"

I've been trying to figure that out myself. I really do wish I could just up and leave like you."

"I had no choice, Tami. We too old for that mess. I will never understand why they do this to the fly ones."

Tami shook her head. "Because they know we the fly ones and that they don't deserve us."

"I must admit, I like this single life. No one to answer to, able to come and go as I please."

"This whole week of the single life. Chile' please." Tami laughed.

I looked out of the window. "I also met someone while I was on the plane."

"And with all that shit you were just talking. Damn, you move quick. What's his name?"

"His name is Que, and, girl, he was too fine. Built like a track star with cinnamon skin, black curls and hazel eyes. We sat next to each other on the plane. He actually helped calm my psycho ass down."

We both laughed. "So what happened next?"

"Well, at the baggage claim, he asked me for my number and offered to show me around town."

"So what did you do? You gave him your number right?" Tami asked, wide-eyed.

"Yes, I did, but I don't feel comfortable going out with him."

"Why not?"

"Because Aaron and I just broke up."

"Jazzy, it's a date. It's not a proposal. Just go and have some fun."

We pulled up to Tami's brownstone and unloaded the car. We walked inside her house. The place reflected Tami's style: tastefully decorated with bright color splotches and ebony furniture. African artwork and gold frames hung from her walls. She led me up the stairs and into her guest bedroom. The room was laid. It has a four-poster, queen size, mahogany bed with two nightstands and a large chest of drawers.

I looked around my room and pulled the rest of my suitcases into the corner of the room. I turned to Tami. "I will be out of here as soon as I can. I already have a couple of places for me to look at."

Tami shook her head and smiled. "This is your room, boo. You can stay as long as you need."

"Thanks for being there for me."

"That's what friends are for. Come downstairs when you're ready." She walked out of the room and then peeked her head back in. "And definitely go out with him. Just see what happens."

I freshened myself up and came downstairs

a couple of hours later. Tami was on her computer. As I walked into the room, Tami called out, "What do you want for dinner?"

"I don't know New York like that. Surprise me."

"There's this Japanese spot called Zenkichi, off of Sixth Street. I can make reservations."

"That sounds pretty good," I replied.

"Okay, then Zenkichi it is." Tami leaned over and dialed on her phone.

Sixth Street was within walking distance from Tami's home.

"The one thing that you'll love about New York." Tami exclaimed as we were seated at our table, "is that everything is in walking distance, especially in Manhattan. When you finally get some of your working affairs in order, I'll finish where Que left off."

I rolled my eyes and laughed. "I'm feeling that." The last time I visited Tami was in 2011 for New Year's Eve, and the most sightseeing I did was looking at the inside of her toilet. I had come down with a crazy-ass case of the stomach flu. Since I decided to make New York my home, I had to know how to maneuver around without her. I picked up my menu and immediately scanned the pages for my favorite dish, tempura.

"Everything here is small plates. We can share if you like."

My phone began to ring. I looked down. It was Aaron. I rolled my eyes and pressed the side button, silencing my phone. Tami looked up from her menu and raised an eyebrow.

"Aaron again?"

"Girl, yes."

"Change your number."

"It's on my to-do list."

Dinner and sake was amazing. I could stay up all night talking to my girl, but I wanted to get an early start on Monday. I had to coordinate flights for when I would have to meet with the partners at Carancel Digital and also make time to find more clients in New York. I kept my phone on silent, opting to use Tami's clock as my alarm. I went to a few freelance website and put in Tami's zip code. A string of jobs popped up under my search. After taking a few cursory glances over the descriptions and the compensation, I smiled. "Ya girl is on the come up."

I fully understood the concept of a New York minute. Everything here was so fast-paced.

I was almost trampled by pedestrians while searching for one of my interviews on Tuesday. Charlotte moved at a snail's pace compared to this. Even Chicago didn't move as fast. My days were consumed with sending proposals to prospective clients, working on projects for Carancel and the occasional apartment hunting. My nights were filled with trying out the different flavors New York had to offer, ignoring Aaron's phone calls and watching Tami do the same with Jordan. My parents and older sisters also reached out to me. However, I had yet to tell them about my recent move. I preferred to keep that under wraps until I was completely settled.

Although Tami repeatedly assured me that I could stay with her, I felt like I needed my own space. I liked a few of the apartments that I had seen, and they were reasonable enough, with prices in the two- to three-thousand-dollar range for a one-bedroom. They were all located in safe neighbors—well as safe as New York could get —but I was still afraid to live alone. It was something that I'd never done before. I knew that I would eventually find one that would speak to me. By the time I was actually able to catch my breath, it was Thursday night and I had not heard from Que. I was a little bit disappointed since he'd made such a big deal of taking me out and showing me the town. I chocked it up to the normal nigga bullshit and began to unwind when I heard my text tone go off.

I looked down at my phone. Under Que's name, it read: "Now that you're all settled in, let's wild out. If you want, I can pick you up, or we can meet up somewhere. Either way it goes, I'm going to see you."

I smiled at the text.

We agreed to meet at Solas at 10 p.m. that Friday. I decided to take an Uber because I didn't want him to know where I was staying. I arrived at the bar at 10:45, precisely on colored people time. Considering it was the early spring, I came out in a peach-colored body con dress with nude Michael Kors Presley pumps. My long hair was pulled into a side part with barrel curls cascading over my left shoulder. I didn't want to lead old boy on, however, I always had to bring my A game. I walked over to the bar and ordered my signature drink, a Madras. As the bartender took my order, I felt an arm gently caress the back of my arm. I turned around and saw that million-dollar grin and those golden-brown eyes. He was looking as devastating as ever. I could see that he'd brought his fly game as well. He was in a cream-colored sports jacket with a wine-colored button-down shirt and dark blue, fitted jeans. The jacket made his skin glow.

"Forget the lady in red; check out the lady in peach. You are absolutely breathtaking."

"Thank you for the compliment. You're looking pretty dapper yourself."

"Did you just say—?" Que questioned.

"It's old Chicago slang, honey," I interrupted.

"So that's where you're from?"

"All day baby. You can see the Chi town swag from a mile away."

"Definitely explains why you caught my eye." He gave me the once over and smiled. "And then some."

I blushed. He continued. "So did you get your famous drink?"

I took a sip of my Madras and smiled. "And what's that?"

"Madras for 800, Jazzy."

"A man that pays attention. Swoon," I said as I leaned into him.

"So how do you like the atmosphere so far?"

"It's pretty dope, very Girls-ish.

"Girls?" he asked.

I smiled and shook my head. "Never mind."

"I meant how do you like New York?" Que asked.

"It's very fast paced and I'm from Chicago. Living in Charlotte didn't help anything."

"Yeah. Charlotte was pretty tough for me to get used to, and I was only there for a few days."

I finished my drink and smiled. Que motioned to the bartender. "One more Madras please, with a gin and tonic."

I set my glass down on the table. "Finally, a man's drank. Put some hair on your balls, man."

Que laughed. "If you only knew."

The bartender gave us our drinks and Que paid. With drinks in hand, we made our way to the dance floor. Between the liquor, dancing and conversation, I was honestly having a great time. We talked about where we grew up, comparing Chicago and New York. Que had never visited Chicago, claiming it was too cold. I explained that it was only cold maybe five months out of the year; otherwise, Chicago was lovely.

After the fourth drink, Que leaned over and whispered in my ear, "I would like to go somewhere a little quieter so I can hear you better."

Knowing where this was headed, I shook my head and smiled. "We can go outside."

He nodded and laughed. "I would like to give you a different type of tour of the city, take you to the real New York."

Maybe it was the drinks, the atmosphere or how incredibly sexy Que looked. Or maybe it was because I didn't want to think about Aaron. Either way, I couldn't resist. I set my empty glass on the speaker.

"Let's go."

CHAPTER 2

Que handed the valet his ticket. The attendant nodded his head and ran off to a far corner of the building. Que stood in front of me and rubbed my shoulders as we waited for his car. My thighs began to tingle. I turned around and the attendant was pulling up in a fly, gunmetal-gray, 2016 Audi A8. The attendant handed Que the keys and then turned around and opened the passenger side door for me. Que tipped him and got into car. And off we went.

Que was speeding like a madman down the strangely quiet streets of Manhattan. Giggling, I chided, "I thought we were sightseeing."

Que laughed. "I know that you've already

seen all of the tourist sites in Manhattan, but there's more to New York than just the city. I'm Brooklyn-born and was raised in Queens. I don't think you've been out that far."

"Well, then show me."

He made a turn from First Street onto the Fifty-Ninth Street. We were heading toward a large bridge. "And now we are on the Queensboro bridge," Que announced.

My eyes lit up, and I took out my phone to take pictures. I was a big Nas fan, and to actually see the famed bridge he devoted so many bars to was absolutely amazing.

"I knew you would like this." As we reached the end of the bridge, Que travelled down a couple of more streets and then hooked a U-turn. We entered the bridge again. I looked over at Que. Perplexed, I asked, "So that was the Queen's sightseeing tour? That was your place that you wanted to show me?"

"Plenty of time for the Queen's tour, Queen. And now I'll show you my place." I saw that we were driving back to Manhattan. After travelling through a maze of high-rises, once again passing Grand Central Station and Bryant Park, Que finally took me to his "place." Driving up to the valet at the Carlyle Hotel, Que placed his car in park. I grabbed my purse as the attendant opened my door and ushered me out of the car. Que wrapped his arm around my waist as we approached the front of the hotel. The door attendant opened the door for us and nodded toward Que. "Evening, Mr. Boudreaux."

I was shocked. Que simply smiled back. "Evening, Jamison."

The place was gorgeous. I guess it was the graphic designer in me, but I've always loved how shades of orange and yellow fabrics and accents provided a contrast against ebony-colored furniture. Sometimes I felt like I should've went into interior design. That might be something that I could do later on. I had time. As we walked toward the elevators, various hotel staff came up to Que, asking him if he needed anything. Upon approaching the elevator, a white-gloved attendant pressed the up button for us. I was speechless. My family wasn't poor; my mother was a doctor and my father was a lawyer. I had stayed in some of the best places all over the world, but this was some next-level shit. I did NOT want to get used to this. A beautiful, blond concierge walked up to Que.

"Monsieur Boudreaux, can I provide you with the usual?"

"Yes," he said and winked at me.

"It will be in your room by the time you arrive."

"Thank you."

The elevator door opened and we stepped inside. The white-gloved elevator attendant nodded his head toward Que.

"Floor twenty-eight, Mr. Boudreaux?"

"Yes," Que answered.

The attendant nodded his head again and pressed the button for the twenty-eight floor. He whispered in my ear to close my eyes. I closed them and felt him place his hands over them.

"This is for good measure. No peeking."

I heard the elevator door open. To keep me from tripping, he held me close and guided me toward the door. I felt him reach into his pocket and then lean over, opening a door. He whispered in my ear again: "Open your eyes."

As he closed the door behind us, I was standing in one of the most beautiful rooms that I had ever seen in my life. Although it was still dark, I had a complete floor-to-ceiling view of Manhattan. A spiral staircase led to the second floor, and on the table was a bottle of Armand de Brignac Brut Gold, two champagne glasses and chocolate-covered strawberries. He took my hand and led me through the living room to the windows. He pointed out the window toward what appeared to be a group of trees about a block away.

"Over there is Central Park."

I stood there thinking, who was this man? How could he afford this room? What did he do? Was it legal? I had to shut off my mind. I was always questioning things instead of going with the flow. But going with the flow also got my heart broken. It made me move to Charlotte; it made me—

"You good?" Que asked. I nodded my head. I was still speechless because of the room, Que, everything. As I stared out the window, I was bound and determined to not let my inner ho out. I was down to give him some, but I wanted him to make the moves on me. I didn't want him thinking the reason I was about to give him some was because I was easily bought and impressed. That was the one thing I was not.

Que took my hand and led me to the couch. He popped open the bottle of champagne and poured a glass. He handed it to me. I already had four drinks at the bar, and I was still feeling buzzed, but I wanted to shut off my mind, so I took a sip. It was utter heaven. Holding up his glass, he said, "I propose a toast. To life, to you, and to new beginnings."

I smiled. "Here, here."

We clinked glasses and drank. I just stared at him. He seemed so natural in this environment. He was a complete contrast to Aaron. Aaron came off goofy and shy but was ultimately a lying-ass dog. Que, on the other hand, came off super smooth, but I caught glimpses of something that I couldn't quite put my finger on. Either way it went, it made my body crave him. After finishing his champagne, he poured another glass and sat closer to me. He reached down and grabbed a strawberry. He traced my lips with the chocolate-covered tip. He then caressed the side of my face and enveloped me in a passionate kiss. As he continued to kiss me, I felt him tug gently at my dress. I pulled back. I totally wanted him, but I had to put up a little more of a fight before I completely gave in. I turned my head away from him as he tried to kiss me again. I scooted away from him, afraid to look up. I didn't want him to be upset.

After a few moments, he tilted my chin up so I could look at him. He smiled warmly. "We are both grown; you knew what it meant to go home with someone after the bar."

"I do but..."

"I don't think you're a ho, Jazmine," Que interrupted. "I already met you, remember, and it wasn't on Tinder. Look, I told you I wanted to show you the real New York, and that's what I did. This hotel we're staying in is the Carlyle Hotel; this room is the Empire Room. Many presidents, celebrities and even Princess Diana have stayed in this hotel."

My mouth dropped open slightly. Que continued. "If you just want to be friends, that's fine. You are tempting, but I like you for you. And I respect you."

I lowered my head, feeling stupid. Not every dude was full of shit. "Thank you for being a gentleman."

He smiled. "It's how I was raised."

I laid my head on his shoulder and looked out the window. New York glittered below me. It was truly the city that never sleeps. As Que rubbed my shoulder, my body began to tingle and throb. It was then that I realized I didn't want to get too much sleep tonight either. I looked up at him and smiled. All of sudden, Que grabbed my chin and consumed my mouth and neck with his lips. His hands roamed and grabbed my body, all of the ample, fleshy parts that I despised. Tug, tug, RIPPPP, and the next thing I knew, I was completely exposed except for my thin pair of Nubian Skin panties. My nipples hardened in the cool air. His eyes became hazy as he stared at me. I felt myself blush and tears sprang to my eyes. I covered my face in complete embarrassment as he removed my undies.

He gently took my hands in his and stared at me. "What's wrong?"

I tried to keep my voice steady. "Why did you look at me that way? I mean I know I'm not the skinniest thing going, but you didn't have to…"

Que put his finger to my lips, shushing me. "Who told you to hate yourself?"

I stared at him. If he only knew. I've always been the kind of chubby girl; I mean at least in my eyes I have. I guess most would say that I

...e in between my legs. I'd never ...fully accept me the way Quinton did. ...med as if he enjoyed every ebb and flow he created in me. The waves within me crashed three times. When he finished, he sat up and stared at me, his manhood at complete attention. I sat up and let my lips travel up his waist, over his chest, finally landing on his full lips. He grabbed a fistful of my hair and brought me to him. I reached down and massaged him before dropping down to my knees and flicking my tongue across his large, swollen head.

My mouth travelled up and down his shaft while his hand remained tangled in my hair. He was so wide and hard, I was bracing myself to be able to take him all in. I wondered if I could. Aaron was not, shall we say, as blessed as him. The thought of Aaron and of Tracy made me lose all inhibitions. I completely lost myself in the moment. I began sucking and massaging even harder, moving my head in all directions, using the texture of my tongue and mouth to please him. His moans of pleasure let me know that I was doing the right thing. As my tongue caressed the vein under his shaft, he pulled me back and laid me down.

had a *King* magazi...
I've had for as long a...
as a big butt and thi...
wearing pants and skirt...
sizes too big. It attrac...
comments from men. This
to develop at ten years ol...
dreams of becoming a prima ...
also kept me from my second l...
The only man I had ever loved also cheated on
me with someone who had the opposite body of
mine. He used to...

Que's voice shook me out of my thoughts.
"Focus on me. Come back to me. Jazzy, you are
one of the most beautiful women I have ever
seen. Solomon described a body such as yours in
his songs. Artists have created some of the most
beautiful works of art from women with your
body. Have you ever seen the Venus De Milo?
You are what a woman is supposed to look like."
With those last words, he began to trace his lips
all over my body, circling around my breasts and
nipples, his tongue caressing my hips and thighs
before he came back up and began to devour
me from below.

Electricity ran through me as he kissed and

circled his tong...
had a man ...
It se...

astic...

He just stared at me and smiled. He softly sang to me, "It seems like you're ready."

I closed my eyes and laughed at him. No, he didn't start singing R. Kelly to me. This fool right here. "You are too…" He then leaned over me and slid himself deep inside of me. My eyes widened and my legs shook as I accepted him. So thick and so hard, he was able to reach every sensitive inch of me. His strokes were rough and commanding. It felt as if he was fucking his way to paradise. With each thrust, my body reciprocated, my hips turning up to receive him. He kissed my neck and swirled his tongue around my nipples, bringing me to the point of complete delirium. Right before I was about to come, he stopped and stared at me. As the feeling subsided, he lifted me up by my back and started short stroking me. I felt my hips swell up, and then the tsunami hit and the waves consumed me.

He lifted himself off my body and dragged his tongue from my lips to my neck and down the middle of my cleavage. He then pulled me up and guided me to the window overlooking central park. It was gradually lighting up. He pushed me up against the window.

"What are you doing?" I asked.

"I want the world to worship your body the way I do," Que whispered in my ear. He then wrapped his arm around my waist, pulling my ass towards him, and entered me from behind. With my hands pressed against the window, Quinton took me from the back, thrusting so hard that it pressed my breasts against the cool window. The sensation of being fucked into oblivion and the coldness of the window was too much for me to bear. I moaned and shook as he grabbed my hair and pulled my head back, giving me a long, deep kiss. As the sun rose, so did I, melting all over Que. He finally allowed himself release as well, grunting and shaking as he climaxed.

He uncoupled from me and led me to the stairs. He pulled me to the king-size bed and laid me down. Grabbing one of my breasts, he leaned down and rolled his tongue over my nipple. He reached his hands between my legs and gently rubbed me. "Just one more," he whispered against my skin, sending shockwaves throughout my body.

It was literally the best sex I had ever had in my life. My body gave out and I went to sleep.

CHAPTER 3

The bright light from the windows brought me out of my slumber. Realizing that I was not at Tami's house, I shot up and looked around. The memories of the early morning began to creep back, as well as the beginning of a hangover. Collapsing against the pillows, I looked for Que, but he was nowhere to be found. Looking at the pillow next to me, I saw a note. Squinting, I brought the letter up to my face.

"My brown-skinned Jazmine,

I left for the day, beautiful. I will be back a little bit later. You can stay as long as you want and order anything that you want, whether it's food or new clothes.

Until then, relax, look out the window and enjoy New York. It's yours for the taking.

Que

I smiled and went back to sleep.

A few hours later, I awoke again and thought about what I wanted for breakfast. Although a day of lounging around in these gorgeous surroundings and eating delicious food certainly sounded amazing, I knew I had to get back to Tami's and work on a few projects. So, putting on my big girl panties, I put on my clothes and left the hotel room. Once outside, I ordered an Uber driver. I had to wait four minutes. I texted Que to let him know I left and to thank him for the wonderful time. A few minutes later, my driver arrived and I got in the car.

Although this was New York, I was not about to walk around in a torn dress, pumps and a jacket in the middle of the day. I had the Uber driver take me to Tami's house so I could freshen up. When I walked in, I was half expecting Tami, who sometimes worked from home, to be sitting in her office, teasing me about where I was last night. She wasn't home. I breathed a sigh of relief.

I ran upstairs to take a shower. I could still smell Que's Gucci Guilty cologne on my skin. I let the warm water run all over my body. After my shower, I changed into a fresh pair of jeans and a T-shirt. Wanting to enjoy the rest of my day, I took my laptop and bag and headed out to one of the local cafes. The sun was shining. As I pulled out my phone to Yelp the nearest café within walking distance, I looked at my phone and noticed that I didn't receive a return text from Quinton. I refused to let that bother me, so I put it out of my head and followed Siri's directions.

After a few minutes, I found myself standing in front of Le Pain Quotidian. Even though it eased up in the shower, I was still suffering from my hangover and knew that caffeine would provide me with that much-needed relief. I ordered a triple espresso. I took my number and headed outside. Once I found a seat, I took out my computer and loaded up my apps. While waiting for my computer to connect to the Wi-Fi, I took out my phone and browsed my newsstand. One story in particular caught my attention.

Ringleader of a high-class Florida theft ring has fled

to New York.

The subheading said, "May be in hiding in plain sight." I clicked on the link and read the story.

The ringleader of a Miami-based theft ring, which targeted wealthy homes in the South Beach area, may have fled to New York to escape the feds.

My coffee arrived. I thanked the waiter and continued reading.

The theft ring was responsible for stealing up to 50 million dollars' worth of artwork and jewelry from some of Miami's wealthiest families. The tipoff regarding the ringleader's identity and potential whereabouts came from a female accomplice in the group, who provided this information in exchange for bond and immunity.

Story still developing.

I shook my head and looked around. They were never going to find this man. It was damn near impossible to find someone in a city of millions. As long as he stayed low-key and changed some things about his appearance, he would be just fine. Even though I was a good girl and was scared to even drive five miles over the speed limit, I always rooted for the bad guy to get away with it. My internet finally connected.

"Okay Jazzy" I said to myself, "back to reality. It's time to work."

I worked until sundown, but I was able to complete a week's worth of work in about three hours. I was completely energized from earlier this morning. I couldn't get over how well he knew my body. It was almost as if we had known each other for years. I looked down at my phone. Still no text. Definitely back to reality. I shook my head and packed up my laptop. Hey, at least I could relax the rest of the weekend. Although I knew I would probably never see Que again, I still couldn't wait to get back to Tami's and tell her all the juicy details.

As I entered Tami's brownstone, I could hear her cussing. I stayed in the dining room, just far enough to give her privacy but just close enough in case I had to help her kick Jordan's ass.

"Who the fuck is she, Jordan?"

"Who the fuck is who, Tami?" Jordan responded sarcastically.

"Nigga, please don't play with me. It would not be in your best interest to play stupid right now. Who is the bitch who keeps texting you?"

"Man, I get texts all the time. I let you see

my shit, so I really don't know what you're talking about."

"Okay, my nigga, let me refresh your memory. Her name is Ariana and she said she missed that good dick last night."

"I don't have no shit like that in my phone, Tami. I let you see my shit all the time. You sure you ain't the one fucking around on me?"

I knew my homegirl, and at that moment I prayed that she wouldn't do anything stupid that would cause her to lose everything. When Tami got silent like this, it was because of one of two things: either she was trying not to cry or she was trying not to bust a nigga's head wide open. Knowing my girl, it was probably the latter. At that moment, I wanted to barge into the room and take her somewhere, but Tami had to handle her business. I continued to stand near the door.

Tami cleared her throat and continued. "You right. She didn't send that to your phone. She sent that bullshit directly to me." I then heard something slide across the counter. I presumed she slid her phone to Jordan so he could read the messages. "Read it for yourself."

"Oh shit."

"Let's read it together, shall we?" Tami cleared her throat. "I don't know how long you've been dating Jordan, but I've been having sex with him for a while. Like four years."

Shit just got real. Tami was not playing. Damn. Gettem, ma.

"Ya know, I thought she was bullshitting. But then she described that mole you got on ya dick and I knew she was telling the truth."

Jordan was silent for a moment. I could literally hear his brain trying to come up with an effective lie.

"You know, I've looked the other way, but this time I—

"Yo, don't let your miserable, single homegirl fuck up what we have."

Brrrepp!!! Excuse me, nigga. I cocked my head to the side, about to barge into the room and pop him upside his head.

"Excuse me. What did you just say?" Tami asked.

"Man, you gonna let Jazzy break us up. Just because your homegirl doesn't have a man, it doesn't mean that you gotta follow suit. Miserable bitches love company." There was silence and then the sound of breaking glass.

"What the fuck?" Jordan yelled.

"We are done. Get out," Tami said in a strange, calm voice. When a woman is fed up…

"Tami, I…" Jordan begged.

"I threw the glass as a warning. If I wanted to hit you, I would have. You have nothing here. There is nothing for you here."

I heard Jordan walk toward the front of the room. He walked past me and left, slamming the door behind him. I walked into the kitchen where I saw Tami staring straight ahead with her hands pressed firmly against the island. When she saw me walk toward her, she smiled and laughed softly. Tears started running down her cheeks.

"How long have you been standing in the next room?" Tami asked.

"I heard everything," I replied.

"I knew you were there. That's why I didn't fire on him. I didn't want you to have to testify against me."

We laughed. I put my arm around my bestie's shoulders and gave her a hug. "You are too fly for that type of shit. You can do better by yourself. We Chicago girls; we don't mess around with broke asses. But I will allow you this one charity case."

Tami laughed and wiped her cheeks. "Where were you last night?"

I took a deep sigh and walked out of the kitchen.

"Oh no. You're not going to leave me hanging like that." Tami followed me into the living room. We sat down on her couch.

"He took me to the Empire Suite."

Tami's eyes widened. "At the Carlyle? Girl, you better had your legs behind your neck for that. That room is fifteen thousand dollars a night."

My mouth dropped open. "Really, Tami? Ho shit? Really?

Laughing, Tami continued. "Even if he had a dick the size of a crayon, this man is a keeper. He already showing you the finest things in life, and honey, you honestly deserve it. We both do."

I nodded. "I never been done like that before. He was literally the best lover that I ever had in my life."

"So what are you going to do?"

"Only time will tell," I answered.

CHAPTER 4

A few days went by and I still hadn't heard from Que. I went back to my regularly scheduled program. I had my first one-night stand, and I realized it really wasn't that bad. Maybe I was one of the lucky ones to not feel regret. I mean, I'd gotten a chance to spend the night in an exclusive hotel with a gorgeous man who showed me the world. I wasn't going to do something like that again, but it was still a nice memory to have. I finally felt like an actual grown-up. I shored up another account with a digital company based in Manhattan. They were affiliated with one of the biggest game companies on the east coast. New York was proving to be a most amazing adventure.

While working on a design concept for Carancel, my phone began to ring. I looked down at the caller ID, and to my surprise, it was Que. I contemplated answering the phone. On one hand, I was beyond excited to talk to him, but another part of me was pissed that he hadn't contacted me in almost a week. The phone rang out. Okay, back to work. The phone began to ring again. He was calling me back. Smiling, I picked it up on the third ring.

"Hello?" I answered calmly.

"Jazzy, I know you probably hate me. I would too if I were you, but I had to fly out right quick to a sales meeting."

"Ya know, when you say sales trip, I think drug dealer."

"No. Never that. I deal…"

"Just what I thought. Goodbye, Que."

I was about to hit the end button when he yelled over the phone. "Come to lunch with me. Please, Jazzy. Hear me out. It was hard to not talk to you. You've been on my mind since I met you on the plane. I just had to handle business. Plus, I didn't want to come off thirsty."

I chuckled to myself. "Yeah, yeah, yeahhh."

Que continued. "Just meet me at Masa, at 12:00 p.m."

I shook my head. "I'll be there." I hung up the phone. I looked at the time and saw it was nine thirty. I would start getting ready around ten thirty or so. Screw it. Who I was kidding? I was too excited, and I needed to find the perfect outfit. I spent about thirty minutes trying to find just the right look for a daytime excursion. I wanted to look nice but not like I was trying too hard. I ended up picking out a black jumpsuit with bright yellow pumps. A gold belt finished the look.

It took about an hour to get ready. Once I was finished, I stepped outside and called an Uber. The driver, a middle-aged Arab man, pulled up four minutes later and opened the door for me.

"It should take about ten minutes to arrive at Masa."

I would be a little bit early. "Thank you."

The driver took the streets to the restaurant. Even in the middle of the day, there were traffic and pedestrians all over. I felt that this congestion was something that I would never ever get used to. We finally pulled up to Masa at

Columbus Circle. I walked inside the restaurant and was in complete awe. While looking at the dark walls and red lamps, my thoughts once again wandered to what Que really did for work. I knew you could do well in sales, but unless you owned the company, you're not going to pull in bank like this. Or maybe he was a trust fund kid. I could understand if he didn't want to tell me right away. He probably just wanted to make sure that I wasn't a gold digger. I have my own, but a girl could seriously get used to this. A waiter came up to greet me.

"You must be Miss Jazmine. We have been expecting you."

I nodded my head.

"Right this way." I followed the waiter to my table, and there was Que sitting across from me, smiling with appreciation. He had already ordered an assortment of sushi and tempura. Que, as always, was looking absolutely gorgeous. He was wearing a fitted black cashmere sweater with a white button-down shirt underneath. He stood up and greeted me.

"You never cease to amaze me. You are stunning." He gave me a quick kiss on my hand.

"Thank you, and likewise."

Que pulled out my chair and I sat down. He sat down on the other side of the table. Reaching down, he pulled out a large box and handed it to me.

"This is for you."

"What is this?"

"Just open it. It's an 'I'm sorry' gift for not talking to you over the last couple days."

I untied the soft black bow and opened up the box. Inside the delicate red tissue paper was a beautiful black silk, Tracy Reese midi dress. It was absolutely amazing and was in my exact size. I'd seen this dress in Nordstrom when I was living in Charlotte, but I couldn't afford the price tag.

"It's beautiful and everything, but I can't accept this. It's too much, and—"

"It's a gift," Que interrupted.

"I understand that, but look." I sighed. "I just got out of a relationship. That is the reason why I left Charlotte. I just really want to focus on me right now, so I'm not really looking for something serious."

Que nodded his head. "I understand. I'm feeling you, but I respect you. Other females would have took the gift and still bullshitted with me, but you're different. And that's why I do what I do for you."

I nodded my head and looked down at my hands.

"I honestly just want your company and to get to know you better. No other pressure."

"I want to know two things though."

"Ask me anything."

"What do you do for a living?"

"I told you I'm in sales."

"You never told me what type of sales."

"Well, I'm not in debt. I can afford nice things and share them with you. And I also invest wisely."

I just stared at him and smiled. I was fighting my suspicions as much as I could. On one hand, we'd only been on technically two dates, so I had no right to really probe like that. But then again, we'd already had sex, and with previous lovers, I knew what they did and more before we got to that level. I was not going to press the issue. I'll just sit back and enjoy his company. However, if things got more serious as time went on, I would need those answers.

"The other question is: How did you know my size?"

Que took a sip of sake and laughed. "I did run my hands and my lips over every inch of you. I have an eye for beauty, and I paid attention to every exquisite detail."

I felt my body become electrified as he stared at me.

CHAPTER 5

The Empire Suite looked even more magnificent in the daylight. From the living room, I got a better view of New York City. As I stood at the window and stared at Central Park, Que came up behind me and pulled the top of my pantsuit down my waist. He cupped my breasts and traced his tongue from my shoulder to my ear. Biting my lobe, he whispered, "It took all of the power within me not to put you on the table and feast on you. But now that you're here with me, you are all mine."

With one quick movement, Que threw me over his shoulder and walked up the spiral staircase to the king-size bed. He threw me down on the soft comforter and pulled my pantsuit off, leaving me in just my panties. Staying fully clothed, he leaned over me and gently kissed my lips and then my chin and my neck. Grabbing my right breast, he looked up at me and slowly licked around the edge of my nipple. I grabbed the back of his head as he moved to the left one and flicked it with the tip of his tongue. My back arched as I stuffed my breast into his mouth. He pulled up, smiling.

"Hmm, that is the sensitive one. Good to know." He continued to lick my nipple with the tip of his tongue as he slid his hand down my panties and started massaging my pearl. I grinded against his hand until I released all over his fingers. Pulling his hand from my undies, he looked up at me and licked his fingers. Lifting myself up, I began to claw at his clothes while I kissed him. Before long I was looking at his lean, muscular body and big, throbbing manhood. I leaned down in the doggy style position and licked along each vein on his shaft before wrapping my lips around his head. Sucking in as much as I could, I moved my mouth up and down his cock, flicking the tip with my tongue. His moans and slight thrusting in my mouth completely turned me on. I stopped sucking him to kiss his hips. I felt him quiver and he laughed.

"Hmmm…" I said. "That is the sensitive spot."

He pulled me up and laid down, protection in hand. I took the condom from him and opened it up. Putting it in my mouth, I leaned over and rolled the condom down as far as I could.

Que moaned. "My pretty little freak."

I sat up and slowly lowered myself onto him. I felt my body stretch to accommodate his thickness, almost arriving from feeling his shaft grind against my pearl. I began to ride him, throwing my head back as I bounced up and down. His hands gripped my hips so tightly that I thought I would bruise. I didn't care. I just had to have him fucking me. He then wrapped his arms around my waist and pulled me to him, putting my left breast in his mouth. As he swished his tongue against my nipple, he bucked his hips, thrusting deeper inside me. I tried to pull back as I came, but he held me close, continuing to suck me. I melted all over him.

With his arms still wrapped around me and dick still inside me, he laid me on my left side and put my leg on his shoulder. He continued to stroke me, making sure to reach every inch of me, while rubbing my pearl. I tried to throw it back at him, but he put his hand around my neck, gently squeezing.

"Just submit to me, my brown-skinned Jazmine." He then pushed me onto my back and started bearing down on me, wrapping his arm around my waist, lifting up my hips so he could thrust deeper inside me. I literally lost count of all the times I climaxed. I felt him grow harder inside me, and then with a final bellow, he quivered and collapsed on top of me. Que turned his face to me and gave me a gentle kiss on the lips. He then closed his eyes.

As I watched him sleep, I thought to myself. I didn't care how ratchet this may sound, but even if I didn't know his occupation, I was still going to keep messing with him. As long as he made my body feel this way, I was going to keep fucking him. My mind was made up. It was about five in the afternoon when we woke up. I got up and took a long shower. After putting on lotion, I walked into the bedroom to put my clothes on. Que pinned me up against the wall and kissed me.

With his lips next to mine, he whispered, "Despite you wanting to take it slow, I am going to miss the hell out of you. I will be seeing you next week when I come back to town."

I smiled at him. "I would like that." I honestly couldn't wait to see him again, but I had to play it cool.

Our second rendezvous the day before made it so much easier to deal with the bitchy director of one of the companies I worked for. When I took on Amsher Media, I had initially met with the CEO of the company. He was actually a pretty cool guy. However, this chick right here was off the chain. In the guise of "critique," she had some sideways comment for every mockup that I showed her, despite getting the initial buyoff from the CEO. I felt that she was being overly critical because she honestly didn't know what she was doing and wasn't qualified for the job. Picking this up, I asked her what she got her degree in. When she told me she had a bachelor's in French literature from a state school, I ended the inquiry with an exasperated sigh. "No wonder!" I said with a smirk. Realizing that I didn't take her too seriously after that, she backed off. I loved being petty.

I arrived at Tami's at about four thirty in the afternoon. As I unlocked the door, I heard Tami straight up getting it in, loud moans and all. Doing my best to ignore this, I walked into her small office, set up my laptop and finished another Carancel Digital project. This went on for another hour before I heard the door open and Tami and the mystery guy coming down the stairs. I peeked around to see who this Rock of Gibraltar was that had my best friend praising God in ten different languages.

As they kissed at the doorway, I laid eyes on literally the second finest man I'd ever seen in my life. My girl seriously had some good taste. He was 6'2" with light brown skin, gray eyes and full lips. Not wanting to look like a crazy-ass stalker, I went back to working on my computer, but I was still ear hustling.

"I had a great time today," Tami said coyly.

"So did I. So I'll be seeing you again, tomorrow," he said.

"Yes, you will, Chris." They kissed again and he walked out of the apartment. Tami closed the door behind her and walked into her office.

"I'm glad you found a new one. Girl, he is fine. Who is he?" I asked.

Unbothered, Tami smiled. "He's a senior associate from another department at Ernst and Young. We've been cool for a couple years and I knew he was feeling me. However, I didn't let him make any moves because I was with Jordan. Now that I'm not, I kind of want to see what's up with him."

"Finally," I said, throwing my hands up in the air, "you have someone on your level. Fine, educated and with money. You definitely deserve this too."

"Yes. It feels good," she said, smiling. "I was always attracted to Chris, but I was loyal to Jordan, even when I shouldn't have been."

"You did the right thing. Karma also brings good things too, and he is definitely a good thing."

"So what about you and Que?" Tami asked.

"I like him, and he knows how to work my body, but I want to take it slow," I answered.

"That's understandable. Take your time, but don't move too slow."

"Well, I've only really seen him twice, and I've fucked him as many times. I don't think that's moving too slow."

Tami laughed. "See, girl, I knew you could be thotty."

"Stop it," I said, grinning.

"Besides, we all need a little maintenance sometimes, even if it's just physical. Just enjoy the ride."

"Girl, I do, very, very much."

And so it began, my first real whirlwind romance.

CHAPTER 6

A lot happened over the next few months, but I must admit that moving to New York was the best decision I had ever made. I literally had everything that I ever wanted. I was able to secure Carancel Digital, Amsher Media and a few other media companies as steady clients. Despite the initial problems I'd had with the director of Amsher Media, I was given a two-year contract with the company, providing them with their copy as well as brand reinvention. I also didn't depend on Uber anymore, finally learning how to navigate the subways. I saved so much money once I bought the monthly Metro card. Other times, Que would pick me up and take me to a new eatery or festival. It was almost like clockwork.

Each week, always on a Friday, we would have our date in the city or in a surrounding borough, and we would always end up back at the Empire Suite to make love. I always wondered why we would stay at the Carlyle. I mean the place was spectacular, but that room was expensive. I thought the money could be put to better use. Each Saturday morning he would leave, letting me have full use of the room for the rest of the weekend. The staff began to know me by name. That was how I knew he wasn't bringing anyone else around.

I was still very interested in finding out what he did for a living. As time went on, I didn't want to get tied up in something that could mess up everything that I had worked so hard for. He was literally spending a minimum of 450 thousand dollars a month on his suite, if he stayed at the Carlyle on a monthly basis. I would try to slide it in during our conversations, and either he would give me vague answers or he would find a way to change the subject. He would still say he was in sales; however, he wouldn't give me the name of the company. Other times, when I would bring it up, I would end up naked on the floor of the Empire Suite, being driven crazy with ecstasy.

While at work, I googled his name and nothing weird came up. He didn't have too much of an online presence, no Facebook or Instagram. I didn't know if that was a good or bad thing. I only searched up until the fourth page in Google search. I didn't want to expose my computer to a virus. Then the thought hit me…could he be FBI or CIA? Possibly, but I didn't know why he couldn't just tell me that. Despite his secrecy toward his employment, he was still a decent guy, and I actually enjoyed his company. Que would sometimes try to overstep his boundaries and push for more, but I held my ground. He would sometimes send text messages talking about how much he missed me. I would ignore them. Truth be told, I missed him too when he was gone, but I still had to think about what I wanted. I was reluctant to give my heart to someone that I was unsure of. I made the mistake of moving to Charlotte for Aaron after three months, and we saw how that turned out. I didn't come to New York for Quinton, but he was very much a part of my experience here.

During one particular date, Quinton tried once again to stake his claim.

"Jazzy, I've been up in you. Let me be with you."

I sighed. "Nigga, is that how? You know what? Fine. I'll do it, if you tell me who you work for. If you do that, then I am all yours and more."

Quinton took a sip of his champagne and tilted the glass toward me. "Touché', you pretty, petty-ass mothafucka. Touché'."

I laughed. That was also the first night I didn't wake up at the Carlyle. Que dropped me off at Tami's at around eleven o'clock. I unlocked the door and walked in. When I heard Chris's favorite song being sung by Tami, I shook my head and went back outside, sitting on the steps.

"Something wrong?" Quinton asked from his car.

"Tami is fucking again, and I don't want to listen to that for the next hour."

Quinton laughed. "That should be us at the Carlyle."

"That has been us for the last eight weeks. We don't always have to end up in bed together."

Quinton got out of his car and sat next to me on Tami's doorstep. "We don't, but don't act like you're not enjoying it."

"I do, but moderation is key."

"Not when it comes to you."

"I need to move out. I'm going to start searching for an apartment again."

"What is your price range?"

"Two thousand five hundred to four thousand a month."

"You should be able to find something in the neighboring boroughs for that. Manhattan is not all of New York, believe it or not."

"I believe it."

Que kissed me on my forehead and put his arm around my shoulder. It was moments like this when I wanted to give in and be his, but I wanted to make sure I was fully healed before I took that step. I didn't want to come to him as half a woman.

"Let's go get some coffee," Quinton said.

"Great idea. And before you ask…no. I'm coming back to Tami's tonight."

"Damn. It was worth a shot."

An hour later, we returned to Tami's house. Quinton gave me a quick kiss on the steps and waited until I was inside before he drove off. I opened up the door to silence. I gave him the thumbs up and he drove off. I shut the door behind me. I felt my way through the dark to find the stairway to get to my room. Expecting Tami to still be up, I took a quick glance in her room. To my surprise and happiness, I found her fast asleep in Chris's arms. She looked so safe, so happy. I smiled to myself. I knew what I had to do.

Going into hyper gear, after about two weeks of searching, I finally found a cute, one-bedroom apartment in the Williamsburg section of Brooklyn. It was a little bit slower than Manhattan but had just the right amount of cool for me with tons of neighborhood bars and other cool hangouts. Another plus was that it wasn't too far from Tami or my clients in Manhattan. When I told Tami, I could tell she was heartbroken and didn't want me to go. But I knew that as she became more involved with Chris, she would need her space for herself. She asked me about Que, and I told her that we were still dating but we hadn't made anything official. Chris, however, was something different. They already had a history as friends; they could only build something from there. Tami ultimately agreed with me and offered to help me move.

I was officially introduced to Chris during a dinner date at Zenkichi. As what all best friends do when they meet the new guy for the first time, I questioned the hell out of him while making thinly-veiled threats about what I would do if he ever hurt her. As far as I could see, he was a good guy and really had her best interests at heart. Throughout the dinner, I could see the chemistry between them. Looking back on my relationship with Aaron, as well as Tami's situation with Jordan, I would often wonder why some things didn't work out, why dope women went through these things with men. Looking at what Tami and Chris were creating put things in perspective. Maybe we went through these things so that when the right one comes along, we would be able to appreciate them and give them what they deserved also. They were embarking on something amazing, and she totally deserved it.

Tami came with me when I signed the lease and dropped the deposit off to the landlord. I gave her a tour of the place. I was to move on the first, which was a week away. Although I had money saved up, the down payment and first month's rent took a big chunk of money out of me. As we were driving back to her house, Tami turned to me.

"What would you rather put the rest of your money on? Your furniture or the way you express yourself?"

"The way I express myself."

"Okay. So, we will go to IKEA, and there is this dope African art spot to pick up some items. The place isn't too far from me."

"I'm starting from scratch. We're not going to be able to fit everything I need for the apartment in your car."

"Don't worry. We got this."

Being the consummate planner, first we stopped by Home Depot so I could buy some paint. I wanted my place to reflect my personality, something that I had not been allowed to do when I lived with Aaron. With Que taking me to some of the most spectacularly decorated locales in New York, I had a plethora of ideas about how I wanted to curate my space. Luckily, my place allowed me to paint the walls as long as they were painted back to white once I left the apartment. Knowing that I would buy black or dark brown furniture, I chose different shades of reds, burgundies and golds. I bought the small cans because I was only going to apply paint on the accent walls. After putting together my furniture, I knew I and whoever helped me would be too lazy to fully paint four different rooms.

Our next stop was **IKEA**. We walked through the three floors of the store. I was able to get my entire bedroom, living room and dining room, as well as some small items for my kitchen and bathroom, for around twelve hundred dollars. The upside of this was that I had saved a lot of money for some really cute stuff. The downside was that I had fifty-seven boxes of furniture that I needed to put together. The last place Tami took me was to the African artwork spot. The minute I walked into the small shop, located in Harlem, I knew I was going to go into debt. It was full of beautiful statues, paintings and masks. Each one was drenched in rich, warm hues from the motherland. The owner of the gallery reminded me of my Nigerian grandmother with her soft, Igbo accent. I ended up purchasing about ten different pieces, some kente cloth and Ankara throw pillows for my couch and armchairs.

Everything was supposed to be delivered Thursday evening. For Friday, I decided to throw a paint and pizza party to help me personalize my place. Tami and Chris offered their services to help me. On Wednesday afternoon, I received a phone call from Que. After almost three months of casually dating, I could say that we were comfortable enough to be able to poke fun at each other from time to time. I started calling him Tommy whenever he would avoid the subject of telling me what he did for a living. And each time he would ask me why I called him that, I would change the subject just like he did. I loved teasing him. At the three-month mark, which was tonight, I decided to tell him why.

"Jazzy?"

"Yes, Tommy?" I said in a monotone.

"You still gonna call me that?"

"Yes, I am."

"When will you stop?"

I paused and then answered, "When you tell me what you do for a living."

"Sales, sales, sales!" he exclaimed over the phone.

I laughed. "Not good enough. However, I will tell you at the three-month mark."

"It will be exactly three months in about two minutes."

I sat up straight. "Are you serious?"

"Yes. I met you on that Charlotte flight at 1:15 p.m. three months ago."

I was speechless. That was literally one of the sweetest things that had ever been said to me. "Okay." I sighed. "Tommy is the character from the TV show *Martin*. Remember him?"

There was silence on the other end of the phone. Que laughed. "Really? I ought a hang up on your ass. I got a job, Jazzy."

I laughed. "You won't tell me where."

"So what do you want to do this Friday? I'm all yours."

"Well, I moved into my new spot and I need people to help me make my house a home."

"I'm at your service."

"That's what I like to hear. So I'll see you at 5:30 p.m. I'll text you the address."

"I'm on it. And what do I get in return?" Que asked.

"I won't ask you about your job for three months."

"It's a deal."

I packed up my final things from Tami's house. As requested, via email, Aaron had sent over my books and other trinkets from the old place a month ago, and they were being stored in Tami's basement. I would have to come back to her house to pick those things up. Tami told me that she would be at my spot at around 4:00 p.m. to help me get started as she dropped me off at my new apartment. I walked into the place; all of my utilities were on. I was finally home. My place was full of IKEA boxes and the few items that were already assembled when they were delivered. I sat on the couch. It was 11 a.m. I had a few hours to make some magic. I took out my computer and began to work.

Tami and Chris arrived at 4:30 p.m., as did the first round of pizza. We decided to paint the walls first so that while the paint was drying we could assemble the furniture. I decided to paint the living room burgundy, the dining room adobe, the bathroom a golden sun color bedroom a beautiful russet. We taped the trim and windows. As we waited for Que to arrive, I contemplated exactly how I wanted to introduce him. I didn't want to introduce him as my friend since he was more than that. However, he also wasn't my boyfriend. At least I didn't consider him to be that. Yes, we saw each other exclusively. I wasn't dating anyone else, and as far as I could see, neither was he. He was very reliable, and I felt that I could trust him.

He arrived at 5:30 p.m. on the dot. The introductions were quick. After niceties were exchanged, we got to work. As the men began to paint the other rooms, Tami gave me the thumbs up sign.

"You need to jump on that. You didn't tell me he was that fly."

I just winked at her and smiled. We finished painting at around 7:30 p.m. and were starving. It was definitely time to take a food break. Over pizza and mimosas, courtesy of Que, Que and Chris decided to put together the heavier items, such as my bed and dressers, after eating so that I wouldn't have to sleep on the floor. As the men built my furniture in the bedroom, Tami and I put together the coffee tables, bookshelves and

TV stand. Tomorrow I was going to buy all my electronics. I needed a TV, Blu-Ray player, sound system and a Bluetooth iPad stereo. If Que couldn't pick it up, maybe I could have it delivered.

Tami and Chris left at 11:30 p.m. Que decided to stay over. As we were making up my bed, I turned to him.

"I know it's not the Empire Suite, but it's still nice."

"Home is where the heart is. Why didn't you let me get some of this for you?"

"Because it isn't your place to do so. You're not my—"

He walked over and kissed me. "That doesn't mean that I can't look out for you. I know you're not a gold digger, so I want to do nice things for you."

I smiled at him. "You've done more than enough for me."

"Let me take care of you," he said.

"Okay. Tomorrow I'm going to Best Buy to purchase my TV and other things I need."

"I got you!" Quinton exclaimed.

I continued. "But first I want you to spend the night. At my apartment. If you want to come with me, you can. That is all I need from you. Just let me lie in your arms, and if you come to Best Buy with me, you can deliver my items to my apartment." I winked at him and left the room. I walked to the bathroom and touched the wall. The paint was dry to the touch. I closed the window and got in the shower. I was sweaty from working and painting. I thanked God that Tami had unpacked my restroom for me. I undressed and got into the shower. I just stood under the water for the first few minutes. The warm water felt great against my skin. A few minutes later, I heard the shower curtain open and a breeze hit my body. My nipples hardened in response and, a few seconds later, were instantly soothed by Quinton's tongue. I let out a soft moan and grabbed the back of his head, pushing my left breast deeper into his mouth. He pushed me up against the walls and started to rub in between my thighs. All the tension was released from my body.

He lathered up my body and pulled me out of the shower. Still wet, he took me to my bedroom and threw me down face-first onto the bed. Holding my head against the pillow, his hands tangled in my hair, he ran his tongue down my spine and bit me on my ass before he sat up.

"I've been needing this all day. Never deny me this again," Que said gruffly as he lifted up my hips and plunged himself deep inside my body. I felt my body widen to accept him. He was as hard as steel. With his left hand still entangled in my hair, he wrapped his right arm around my waist and placed his hand in between my legs, rubbing me. His strokes were rough, almost angry. He grunted and groaned as he thrust, which brought me beyond the horizon of pleasure. It felt wonderful to be craved, to be someone's addiction.

He whispered in my ear, "Sing me your siren song. Let me crash in you."

Que pressed down and rubbed my pearl as he thrusted deeper inside me. I lost control and was submerged into the warm abyss of pleasure. As I shook and moaned, so did he, and I felt his manhood throb, releasing all the pent-up tension from the last couple of weeks. He fell asleep inside of me.

I awoke in the morning, alone in my bed. Quinton was nowhere to be found. I didn't know whether to be upset or just suck it up and be cool about it. I honestly couldn't be mad at him. Que wasn't my boyfriend; I had made that perfectly clear. I got up and put on a pair of shorts and a tank top. I had to finish unpacking my clothes so I could be ready for a few meetings I had on Monday. I also needed to schedule an Amazon Fresh drop off so I could have some food for the rest of the week. I was opening up my suitcases when I heard my door open. I looked around for a weapon, but the only thing I had was a wire hanger. I was a dead one. First full day on my own and I was gonna die.

A familiar voice called out. "Jazzy?" Que yelled. "You didn't have any food, so I went down the street to buy some breakfast." I smiled to myself.

We ate breakfast in the middle of my living room. He brought me an egg white omelet with spinach, tomatoes and turkey sausage and fresh-squeezed orange juice. After breakfast, we put together the dining room table. I also finished putting away my clothes. I made a list of the additional things I needed for the house. I had already bought most of what I needed from IKEA and just needed to unpack them. I estimated that by Sunday, my house would be completely together.

I got on my computer and ordered my items from Best Buy for same-day pickup. My items would be ready in two hours. As we waited for the order pickup email, I unpacked my dishes. Forgetting that I didn't have dishwashing liquid, I ended up using my shower gel to rinse the dishes off. Que laughed at me as I washed dishes.

"Resourceful. I like that."

I threw a wet napkin at him and smiled. It took two hours to wash and put all of my kitchen items away, and once that was done, my email alert dinged on my phone. My order was ready for pickup. Changing into a pair of pants and a hoodie, Que and I got into his car and left for Best Buy. I was so happy that I was able to fit the items into Que's car. While I was there, I picked up an antenna so I could get the local news on my smart TV. I unlocked the door to my apartment and held it open as Que brought in my TV. In the middle of the living room floor were the four boxes that had been stored in Tami's apartment, as well as my art purchases and a note. I walked over and picked the note up.

I told you giving me a copy of your keys would be worth it. This is one less thing for you to worry about. Que is pretty dope; you should definitely reconsider your position in the future.

Talk soon honey.

Tami

I looked at Que as he brought in the last of my items. I did really enjoy his company. I just might reconsider my position after all. I sat in the middle of the floor and opened up the boxes. I organized my books; I had everything from Toni Morrison to Ta-Nehisi Coates to Colson White-head. I also placed my various statues, including those of Oshun, Oludamare and the Jesus statue I'd bought when I did a semester abroad in Brazil. It was all coming together. As I opened up the last box and emptied it, I found something at the bottom of the box. I picked it up and became enraged. Aaron had conveniently snuck a picture of me and him into the bottom of the box. I took it out and began to rip it up. Que came over to me and put his arms around my waist.

"Are you okay?" he asked.

"Yes I am," I answered and sat down on my couch. Que bent down and picked up a piece of the photo.

"So that's him?" He looked up at me. "You wouldn't react that way if you didn't still have some feelings."

"It's not that. It's just that he won't leave me alone. He still calls me ten times a day and I ignore him. It's like picking at a wound. Healing, but it's slower than it should be. That's part of the reason why I'm so hesitant with you. I don't want to put you in this situation until it's completely solved."

"This can be easily handled," Que said angrily.

I was slightly startled. "I know. I can just change my number, but it's all I have as my connection to Chicago. I shouldn't have to change my number just because some stupid nigga can't get over the mistake he made."

Que sat down next to me. "I agree, but you moved all the way from Charlotte to make a new start. The phone number should be next too."

I looked at him and smiled. "I'll take care of it tomorrow."

"Let's finish this," Que said. He kissed my forehead and got up. I followed. I threw the photo in the trash. A couple of hours later, we were finished and exhausted. As we lay on my bed, Que turned to me. "I want you to wear that dress I bought you. You deserve a much-needed break. I'll take care of the rest of the details. Just get beautiful." I smiled.

Que stood up. "I'll be back here by 8 p.m. Be ready."

I nodded my head and fell asleep.

When I woke up, it was 6:30 p.m. I had an hour to get ready. I took a long shower to soothe my aching muscles. I took out the Tracy Reese dress, and just as I thought, the dress looked and felt like a dream. It hugged every curve perfectly without riding or bunching up in the back. You do really get what you pay for. I paired the dress with a pair of hot pink stilettos and a matching clutch. I put my hair up into a top bun and finished off the look with pink gloss and silver Tiffany studs.

Que arrived at exactly eight o'clock. As I opened the door, I was completely awestruck by how gorgeous he looked. He was in a gray, collarless suit with a cream-colored, button-down, silk shirt. The suit was tailor-made for his body. The gray made his light brown eyes glow. I could tell he was equally impressed as his eyes scanned every inch of my body in this dress.

"God exists. Because it is by his divine power that I don't rip your dress off and fuck you in the middle of your living room."

"It's not because the dress cost as much as a small island?" I asked.

"Money is nothing. I deny myself immediate gratification so that when I do finally get it, it's that much sweeter, that much more intense."

My body became enveloped in goosebumps. "Let's go, shall we?" I said as I closed the door behind me and walked to his car. After he opened my door and ensured I was inside safely, we made our way to Manhattan to the Ponty Bistro. As we got out of the car, I asked him what type of cuisine this was.

"It's a surprise," Que answered.

We walked through the door. After we were seated, I took a glance at the menu, and a smile came to my face. It was West African food. I looked up at him.

"How did you know this was my favorite food?"

"I remember one time you telling me that your dad was Nigerian, so I wanted to wait for a special occasion to take you to this place. Moving out on your own and actually being able to afford a decent spot in New York by yourself is a huge accomplishment. I wanted you to know you're fly."

"Thank you," I said, blushing.

"So have you ever been to Nigeria?"

"When I was younger, but I don't quite remember the trip though. I plan on going back one day. Soon."

"Maybe I can go with you."

"Maybe," I said, smiling.

After finishing our sumptuous meal, we returned to Quinton's car. "You know, we can go back to my place."

"Nope," Quinton answered. "Back to my place. I have a feeling you're not going to want to come back for a while."

The Empire Suite was still as beautiful as ever. I stood in the living room and watched the lights of New York twinkle like small diamonds. Quinton handed me a glass of champagne. I took a sip.

I felt the warmth of his body against me.

"The sky is the limit," he whispered against my neck.

I had to agree. New York had definitely changed my life. In one smooth move, Quinton unzipped my dress. I felt the sleeves fall from my chest as the dress became a crumbled heap at my feet. I turned around and faced him. His eyes devoured my naked body. Taking my hand, he led me to couch and sat me down. Kissing my lips, he reached over for the Armand de Brignac champagne and poured it all over my chest. The sensation of the champagne bubbles and his tongue against my nipples caused my body to grow wet with anticipation. After licking up the last drop of champagne from my breasts, he traced his tongue up my neck and devoured my lips. I undressed him quickly and threw his clothes to the side. As I was reaching down to grab him, he took both of my arms and pinned them against the couch.

"Sometimes you have to let someone else have control, Jazzy."

While still holding my arms, he kissed down my stomach until he found my center. He gently teased my lower lips with his tongue. I tried my best to free myself from his grip as he licked and kissed me. With him continuing to restrain me, all I could do was grind my hips against his mouth as he brought me to climax. Once I was finished, he pulled my hands over my head and held them against the pillow. Holding himself steady with his right hand, he kissed me and roughly pushed himself inside me. I moaned into his mouth as he filled up my body. His hand then traveled up my hip, over my breast and found my neck.

"Submit, Jazmine. Allow someone else to have control."

He held me down as he stroked, staring into my eyes, barely blinking. I couldn't describe the look on his face. It was a mixture of determination and something else that I couldn't quite put my finger on. I struggled, wanting to wrap my arms around him, to caress him. However, the harder I fought, the more he held me down. He continued to bare down on my body. Every nerve was set ablaze as I felt him slide in and out of me. Staring deep into his eyes, I wrapped my legs around him to pull him in.

It was then that I saw something break within him. His face softened and his movements became gentler. He moved his hand from my neck and moved it up to my face, caressing it. He let go of my wrists, and I instinctively caressed his face and wrapped my other arm around him. My hips found his rhythm and we rocked our way to ecstasy. After the tide crashed, we fell asleep in each other's arms.

I woke up a couple hours later. It was still dark outside. Quinton was nowhere to be found. I adjusted to my surroundings. I looked up to the second floor and saw that the bathroom light was on. He was still here. Good. I reached over and poured myself a glass of orange juice. I turned on the TV and turned the channel to ABC. It was 1 a.m. and they were showing the reruns of the previous night's news. As I was listening to the weather, a breaking news story came across the screen. It was a continuation of the news story that I read a couple months ago about the Florida theft ring. With all that was going on over the last few months, I hadn't been able to keep up with anything pop culture or newsworthy, let alone this story. I set my glass on the coffee table and turned up the volume.

"A member of the Florida theft ring that was respon-sible for stealing approximately 50 million dollars' worth of jewelry and rare artwork from some of Miami's

wealthiest families has been released from prison today after disclosing the identity and the potential whereabouts of the leader of the group. The leader, Evan Miles, has been the mastermind of more than fifty burglaries in the South Beach community. Here is a picture of Evan Miles."

My heart stopped as I looked at the picture of the ringleader. No, it couldn't be. I closed my eyes really tightly and then opened them again. It was. It was Quinton. In the picture, his hair was a little longer and he had a large beard. He was definitely heavier than what he was now, but there was no denying it. It was Quinton.

The reporter continued. *"We have been tracking this story in the news because authorities believe the suspect is in hiding in the Greater New York area. Evan Miles may have altered his appearance, and he doesn't have any distinct characteristics to make him identifiable. He is believed to be armed and dangerous. If you have any information, please call Crime Stoppers at one eight hundred, five five five, eight zero one one."*

I glanced up at the spiral staircase. The bathroom light was still on. I was wondering what was taking him so long. I began to get scared, so I turned off the TV and sank back into the couch. The air suddenly got cold and I was shivering. I could not afford to get sick, and I could not afford to get in trouble. I couldn't get over the fact that I was potentially fucking a wanted criminal. I didn't want to go down for his bullshit. I mean the similarities were there: he had the same golden-brown tiger eyes and full lips. They looked remarkably similar, almost like twins, but I refused to give in to the stereotype that all black people looked alike.

I tried to rationalize this as much as I could. My heart refused to believe it was him. I was thinking that maybe I had drunk too much and it had affected my sight, but my brain already accepted the fact. It now all made sense why would he wouldn't tell me who he worked for or what he really did. Why did I always pick the wrong ones? I got everything else right. The right degree, the right career, even the right apartment, but never the right man. I lost my heart when I got with Aaron, now I might lose everything else if I was tied to Quinton or Evan or whatever his name was. Que was still in the bathroom as I ascended the spiral staircase and walked into the bedroom. I stared at the bathroom.

"So you finally woke up Jazzy?" Que called out from the bathroom.

"Yes," I said, startled.

"I'm about to get into the shower."

Trying to keep my voice steady, I said, "Okay."

Que turned on the shower. I had to keep things normal and I had to bide some time. So I walked into the bathroom and got into the shower behind him. Turning him around, I grabbed his manhood and began to stroke it.

"I just need to have another taste of you. Now it's your turn to let me be in control. Don't hold back." I got on my knees and began to suck him. It only took a few minutes before he pulled himself out of my mouth, stepped back and released. I stood up and wiped my lips. I smiled at him. "Proceed."

I stepped out of the shower, wrapped myself in a robe and walked back into the bedroom. I had to silence my heart. Sitting on the bed, I looked over and stared at the closet. I had to find some clue that the news was wrong, that my mind was wrong. I walked over to the closet and opened the door. Looking past my dress, his clothes and our shoes, I saw a safe in the corner of the closet. I had to make this quick. I didn't have too much time.

I turned around towards the bathroom. The shower was still running. I turned back around and tried to fiddle with the lock. It would not move. Maybe he wasn't using this for anything. All suites had a safe in their room. This didn't mean anything. But I just couldn't stop trying to open the safe. If there was nothing to hide, it wouldn't be locked. But it was locked, so there must be something in there. My brain started screaming to me, "Jazzy, you don't need any more evidence. You have the picture. You have the news story. What more do you need? You are not the cops. This is not your job. Jazzy…"

All of a sudden, the voice calling my name in my head took on a masculine tone. "Jazzy?"

I froze. Oh. My. God. I was caught. I turned around. There was Quinton in only a towel, looking as beautiful as ever, standing at the bathroom door.

"Jazmine, did you find what you were looking for?" He crossed his arms and leaned against the doorframe. His golden-brown eyes were searching mine.

I stepped away from the closet and took a deep breath.

"Jazzy? Did you find what you were looking for?" He took a step towards me.

I was frozen. I couldn't move. As they say, curiosity killed the cat. And unfortunately, I may be next.

FIND out what happens next in Loving The Wrong Man Book 2! Available Now!

FOLLOW Mia Black on Instagram for more updates: @authormiablack

Made in the USA
Lexington, KY
22 June 2019